D0574501

EVERYBODY GETS THE BLUES

Leslie Staub   Pictures by R. G. Roth

Harcourt Children's Books
Houghton Mifflin Harcourt
Boston New York 2012

Harcourt Children's Books is an imprint of Houghton Mifflin Harcourt Publishing Company.

www.hmhbooks.com

The illustrations in this book were hand drawn, combined with collage, and then designed in Photoshop.
The text type was set in Le Havre Rounded.   The display type was set in Carrotflower.
The title type was designed and hand-lettered by R. G. Roth.
Design by Regina Roff

LIBRARY OF CONGRESS CATALOGING-IN-PUBLICATION DATA
Staub, Leslie, 1957-
Everybody gets the blues / written by Leslie Staub ; pictures by R.G. Roth.
p. cm.
Summary: Simple, rhyming text reveals that "Blues Guy" visits everyone now and then, from rodeo clowns to scary bullies.
ISBN 978-0-15-206300-9   [1. Sadness—Fiction. 2. Blues (Music)—Fiction.] I. Roth, Robert, 1965- ill. II. Title.   PZ8.3.S797Eve 2012   [E]—dc22   2010043400

Manufactured in China   LEO 10 9 8 7 6 5 4 3 2 1
4500319744

For Mary Boyd, who was living proof
of the power of kindness
—L.S.

For Tash and Gray-go,
love, Daddy
—R.R.

Sometimes I'm happy

under the great blue sky.

Other times,

I Cry and Cry.

And it's . . .

I feel all bad and mad and sad inside."

Tears well up in his kind dark eyes.

He takes out his hanky and says with a sigh,

"Everybody gets the blues sometimes:

the boo-hoo blues,
the you lose blues,
the oh no, don't go, miss you blues."

Blues Guy sits there by my side,

sometimes talking, sometimes quiet.

He doesn't make me do a thing.

That is how it is with him.

We sit together,

and then . . .

We Sing:
"I've got the blues so bad,
I want to cry, cry, cry,
I feel so bad and mad and sad inside!"

We sing so loud, we start to rise.
We rise so high, we start to fly—

we fly to where someone else is crying.

Everybody gets the
blues sometimes:
moms and dads,
dogs and cats,

rodeo clowns in silly hats,

scary bullies,

beauty queens,

little old ladies from New Orleans,

tiny babies, big kids too.

Everybody gets the blues.

Do you?

We sing our blues
sweet and slow
for everyone who's feeling low.
With every breath, with every note
we send our love—

"You're not alone!
Everybody gets the blue-Woo-Woo-Wooze.
Everybody gets the blues."

When we notice tears have passed,
our hearts are light, the sky is vast!
Then it's time to say goodbye.

Goodbye, Blues Guy.

I'll see *you* some other time."